For my husband Adam who is my inspiration in all things.
Thank you for always believing in me.

To those who volunteer their time, money and resources to animals
in need, to those that protect them, love them and fight for them...
this book is dedicated to you.

A portion of proceeds from every sale of this book
will be donated to animals in need.

Lacey L.Bakker

Pandamonium Publishing House

Panda the Very Bad Cat

ISBN: **978 0 9952955 0 6**

Design: Jason Buhagiar
Cover Design: Jason Buhagiar

Published and Printed in Canada.

Panda
the Very Bad Cat

PANDA

written by

Lacey L.Bakker

illustrated by

Jason Buhagiar

Panda the cat was a very bad boy;

he loved to find mischief more than a toy.

He loved to cause chaos and mayhem at home.

He wasn't a kitten but not fully grown.

He jumped onto the table and into some paint;

he thought that his human was going to faint.

He left purple paw prints all over the place.

He pulled on the tablecloth and splashed milk on his face.

Panda jumped on the counter and ate all that he could;

his human kept pleading, "Please Panda! BE GOOD!"

He knocked over pans and a carton of eggs; he was covered in bacon from his nose to his legs!

He crawled on his belly through some sparkles and glue.

He rolled on his back and spilled juice on a shoe!

He swung from the fan on the ceiling up high;

he didn't stop there because he thought he could fly!

His human looked frazzled and begged him to freeze,
but Panda just giggled and ran past her knees!

He ran to the front door and let in a frog.

He sneezed on the goldfish and coughed on the dog

He almost escaped through the front door with glee,

but there stood his human-he had nowhere to flee!

She scooped up the bad cat with all of her might;

Panda knew what was happening and put up a fight.

He launched from her arms and into the air,
he grabbed onto the curtains but didn't stop there!

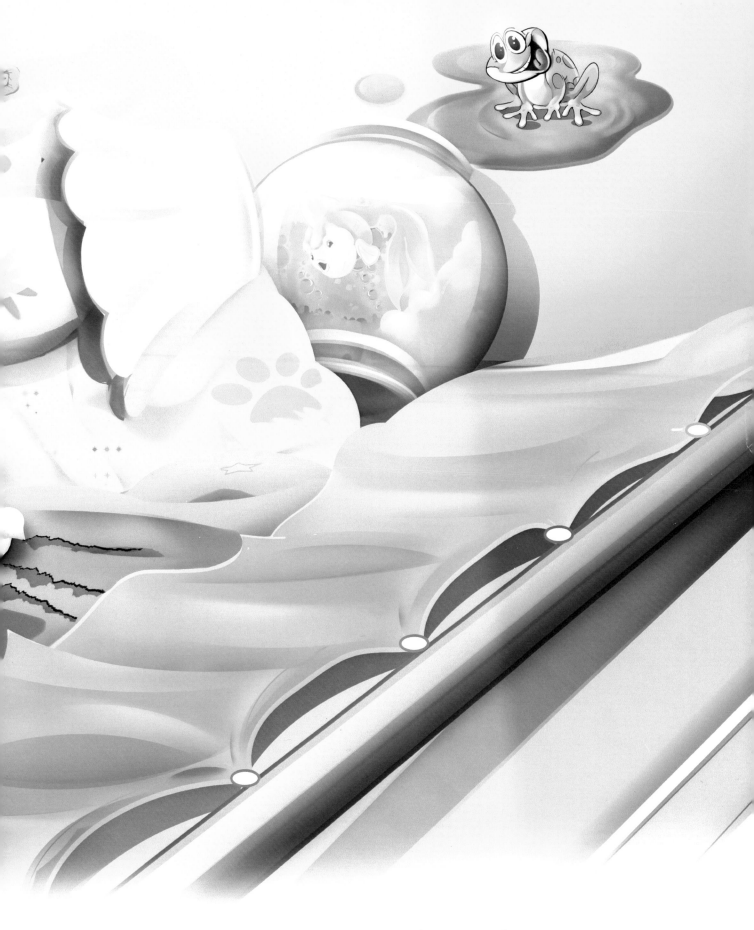

He slid down the curtains and tore them in two;
he knocked over the lamp and the goldfish bowl too!

He tried to climb up the bookcase with speed,

but the bookcase tipped over and scared him indeed!

His human was angry, and she headed straight toward him.

She stretched out her arms and just about grabbed him.

Panda jumped on the coat rack and over a rug,

he landed on all fours on the floor of the tub.

He had been defeated and now was all wet.

This wasn't Panda's last adventure-on that you can bet!

Panda the cat is inspired by a real cat

who loves to find mischief more than a toy.

The real Panda belongs to the author's dad Eric who lives on a farm in Canada.

www.thekittycatclan.com